For Alison Inches, the best editor in town—S.H.
For Susanna—T.L.

VIKING
Published by the Penguin Group
Penguin Books USA Inc., 375 Hudson Street, New York, New York 10014, U.S.A.
Penguin Books Ltd, 27 Wrights Lane, London W8 5TZ, England
Penguin Books Australia Ltd, Ringwood, Victoria, Australia
Penguin Books Canada Ltd, 10 Alcorn Avenue, Toronto, Ontario, Canada M4V 3B2
Penguin Books (N.Z.) Ltd, 182–190 Wairau Road, Auckland 10, New Zealand

Penguin Books Ltd, Registered Offices: Harmondsworth, Middlesex, England

First published in the United States of America by Viking,
a division of Penguin Books USA Inc., 1995

Published simultaneously in Puffin Books

1   3   5   7   9   10   8   6   4   2

LIBRARY OF CONGRESS CATALOGING-IN-PUBLICATION DATA
Hunter, Sara Hoagland.
Miss Piggy's night out / by Sara Hoagland Hunter;
illustrated by Tom Leigh.   p.   cm.—(Viking easy-to-read)
Summary: When their dinner at a fancy restaurant ends in embarrassment
for Miss Piggy, Kermit tries to make her feel better.
ISBN 0-670-86107-3. — ISBN 0-14-037556-2 (pbk.)
[1. Restaurants—Fiction.   2. Puppets—Fiction.]
I. Leigh, Tom, ill. II. Title. III. Series.
PZ7.H9185Mi 1995 [E]—dc20   95-16711 CIP AC

Printed in the United States of America   Set in New Baskerville

Reading level 1.6

Miss Piggy's Night Out

by Sara Hoagland Hunter
illustrated by Tom Leigh

VIKING

Miss Piggy wanted to eat out.

Kermit wanted to read his book.

"All the stars eat at Cloud Nine,"

said Miss Piggy.

"Do you think I am a star?"

Kermit did not answer.

"Well, do you?"

Kermit closed his book.

"Yes," he said.

"All the stars eat at Cloud Nine,"
said Miss Piggy again.

"Then you will eat at Cloud Nine,"
said Kermit.

"What a good idea!" said Miss Piggy.

Miss Piggy asked for the center table.

"A star must be seen," she said.

They sat down.

"Do I look like a star?"

asked Miss Piggy.

"Yes," said Kermit.

They ordered hot chocolate.
Miss Piggy asked for lots of
whipped cream.

"Oh, I can't
drink all that,"
she said.

But she did.
In a jiffy.

"My, that was good!" said Miss Piggy.

"Maybe I will have another one."

Kermit looked at Miss Piggy.

He looked again.

"What are you staring at?" she asked.

"Your…" began Kermit, pointing at
Miss Piggy's nose.

"What?" asked Miss Piggy.

She turned around.

"There's Mr. Big!" shouted Miss Piggy.

Kermit did not see Mr. Big.

He was looking at Miss Piggy's nose.

There was whipped cream on it.

PCH

Cuéntame tu Historia

It was a *big* blob of whipped cream.

Kermit tried to tell her.

Miss Piggy did not listen.

"Mr. Big makes movies," she said.

"I want to be his new star!"

Miss Piggy talked and talked.

The blob on her nose moved up and down.

"I must meet Mr. Big!" said Miss Piggy.

She stood up.

"Stop!" cried Kermit.

Miss Piggy stopped.

A waiter stopped too.

"May I help you?" asked the waiter.

Then he saw Miss Piggy's nose.

He dropped his tray.

Dishes crashed!

Food flew!

"*He* knows I am a star," said Miss Piggy.

She smiled at the waiter.

Then she turned to Kermit.

"My dress is a mess.

What will Mr. Big think?"

"The problem is not your dress,"

said Kermit.

"It is your nose."

Miss Piggy did not listen.

"Look, Kermit," she said.

People were pointing at Miss Piggy.

"I am a star."

Miss Piggy waved.

"Hello, fans!" she said.

Everyone laughed.

What was Kermit to do?

He had an idea.

If he rubbed his nose,

maybe Miss Piggy would

rub her nose too.

It did not work.

"Stop rubbing your nose," said Miss Piggy.

"What will my fans think?"

Just then, Mr. Big turned around.

He looked right at Miss Piggy.

Kermit threw a napkin

over Miss Piggy's face.

She took it off.

"Don't try and hide me!" she said.

"I am a star!"

"I give up," said Kermit.

"He sees me!" said Miss Piggy.

"I must go to him."

They went to meet Mr. Big.

Miss Piggy winked at Mr. Big.

Mr. Big stared at her nose.

His eyes grew bigger and bigger.

"I am Miss Piggy," she said.

"I am a star!"

Miss Piggy moved closer.

Mr. Big moved away.

"I want to be in your next movie,"

she said.

Mr. Big laughed.

He handed Miss Piggy a mirror.

She looked into the mirror.

She saw her nose.

Miss Piggy ran out of Cloud Nine.

She ran all the way home.

Kermit ran after her.

He knocked on her door.

"Why didn't you tell me

I had whipped cream

on my nose?" she asked.

"I tried," said Kermit.

"I'm never coming out,"
said Miss Piggy.
"You have to come out,"
said Kermit.
"Your fans need you."

Miss Piggy was out in a flash.

"Fans?" she asked.

"Where?"

"Right here," said Kermit.

He pointed to himself.

"I am your biggest fan."